This Book
Was Donated By

Amanda
Frick

Summer Reading Club
2000

THE LINE UP BOOK

MARISABINA RUSSO

 Greenwillow Books, New York

Printed in Hong Kong by South China Printing Co.
First Edition   10 9 8 7 6 5

The full-color art work, gouache paintings, were mechanically separated
and reproduced in four colors. The text typeface is Avant Garde Book
and the display type is Roslyn Gothic Bold.

Library of Congress Cataloging-in-Publication Data

Russo, Marisabina.   The line up book.
Summary: Sam lines up blocks, books, boots,
cars, and other objects, all the way from
his room to his mother in the kitchen.
[1. Play—Fiction]   I. Title.
PZ7.R9192Li 1986   [E]   85-24907
ISBN 0-688-06204-0
ISBN 0-688-06205-9 (lib. ed.)

For Whitney, Hannah, Ben,
and of course, Sam

Sam dumped all his blocks on the floor.

Then he heard his mother calling him for lunch.

"Just a minute," Sam called back.

Sam started to line up his blocks. They stretched
all the way across his room and out the door.

When he ran out of blocks, Sam said,
"I need something else."

Books! The books lined up all the
way to the bathroom.

"Come on, Sam," he heard his mother
calling.

"Just a minute," Sam called back.
He looked around.

"I need something else," said Sam.

Bath toys! Now the line reached the front door.

"Sam, it's time to wash your hands," called his mother.

"Just a minute," Sam called back.

The bath toys were all used up.

"I need something else," said Sam.

Boots! The boots lined up right into the living room.

"Sam, the soup is getting cold," called his mother.

"Just a minute," Sam called back.

"I'm almost there."

He looked around the living room.

"I need something else," said Sam.

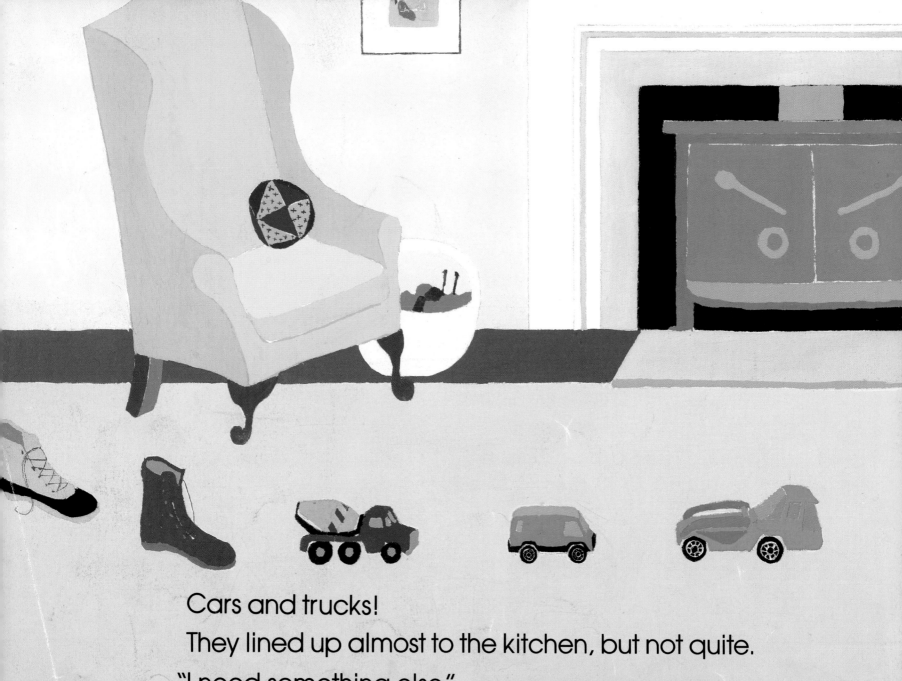

Cars and trucks!

They lined up almost to the kitchen, but not quite.

"I need something else."

"Sam, I'm going to count to three," called his mother
in a louder voice.

"No, wait! Just a minute," called Sam.

Sam looked all around.

There were plenty of things to line up in the living room, but either they were up too high, or too heavy, or not to be touched by Sam.

"I've got to find one more thing," said Sam. "I'm almost there."

"One," counted his mother.

"I need something else," said Sam.

Then Sam had an idea.

"Two . . . ," said his mother.

He lay down on the floor with his hands over his head.

Sam just reached the kitchen.

He looked up and there was his mother saying,
"Three!" She looked down at Sam.
"What are you doing?" she asked.
"I made a line all the way from my room to you!"
said Sam.

His mother looked at the line. She picked Sam
up off the floor and hugged him.

"It's terrific," she said.

Sam smiled.

"But next time, please come when I call you."

"I love you, Mama," said Sam.

"I love you, Sam," said his mother, "and now
it's time for lunch."